James Inglis

Tirhoot rhymes

James Inglis

Tirhoot rhymes

ISBN/EAN: 9783337261061

Printed in Europe, USA, Canada, Australia, Japan

Cover: Foto ©Andreas Hilbeck / pixelio.de

More available books at **www.hansebooks.com**

Tirhoot Rhymes.

BY

"MAORI."

WYMAN & Co., PUBLISHERS, CALCUTTA.

1873.

CALCUTTA :

CALCUTTA CENTRAL PRESS COMPANY, LIMITED,
5, COUNCIL HOUSE STREET.

PREFACE.

I HAVE no pretensions to be a poet. I have been asked by many personal friends to publish these pieces, and somewhat against my own judgment I have consented to do so. Full of imperfections as they are, I hope that no unfriendly eye will look upon these pages. They are meant for my friends alone; and if any of the pieces or songs will recall happy evenings spent long ago, or if they even call up a passing smile or give rise to a kindly thought, they will have succeeded in accomplishing all I could ever have hoped for them.* A few notes accompany some of the pieces, explaining the circumstances under which they were written. Some are now published for the first time; others have already appeared in various papers and magazines at Home, in New Zealand, and in India. I dedicate this book, in all diffidence, to my fellow planters of Tirhoot, Chumparun, and Chupra, among whom I count some of my warmest and dearest friends.—*Bus.*

JAS. INGLIS.

* I believe there is an idea obtaining among some, that a planter ought to have no thought beyond "The Shop;" but we think (I speak for planters) that the old proverb—" All work and no play makes Jack a dull boy"—applies equally to us as to other classes, and we quite fail to see the heinousness of, at odd times, singing, or even composing a song.

INDEX.

— • —

ii

Tirhoot Rhymes.

THE GHOST OF INVERMARK.

INVERMARK CASTLE is a fine, old, feudal ruin, on the North Esk, near the top of Lochlee, in Forfarshire. At one time it was supposed to be haunted by a white lady. The discovery of the Ghost, as it actually occurred, is related in the following lines. They were published some years ago in *Indian Society*—a journal started in Calcutta, but which died in early childhood.

IT was a lordly Castle in the olden time,
    Rearing its battlements against the hill;
Where crimson heather, in its blushing prime,
    (Wooed by the murmur of the laughing rill),
Scattered its perfume at the early chime,
        When all was still.

Lights from the casements gleamed at night,
    From huge fires blazing in the lofty hall;
And men-at-arms, with burnished steel bedight,
    Full many a deed of daring would recall;
And swords, and battle-axes, keen and bright,
        Flashed on the wall.

The wandering minstrel raised a martial strain;
    And as he sang the stirring deeds of yore,
The rude retainers caught the wild refrain,
    And roused the sleepers on the oaken floor,
Who started, yawned, then went to sleep again,
               Perchance to snore.

The great gaunt boar-hound stretched him on the hearth,
    The huge fire roaring like a blacksmith's bellows,
All was wild revelry and noisy mirth ;
    For, as our pedagogues and grand-dads tell us,
There lived not then upon the earth
               More reckless fellows.

But when my story opens, all was changed ;
    For e'en the waving heather was no more :
And where the lordly stag had erst while ranged,
    The golden barley, promised ample store ;
And antiquaries prosed, as if deranged,
               O'er signs of yore.

Great gaping fissures in the walls were seen;
    The night winds whistled o'er the ruins grey ;
And ivy rustled, where the tapestry had been—
    The clinging ivy—wedded to decay ;
And sculpture, dank and mossy green,
               Now mouldering lay.

Full many a merry night the bats had there;
    The sly moon peeping from behind a cloud ;
Grave frogs held council on the shattered stair,
    Where once had trod the " gay and giddy crowd",—
Baron and lord, gay knight, and lady fair,
                And prelate proud.

The shepherd, when he neared the ruined keep,
    Would tremulously whistle, hum, and haw ;
And trembling, hurry up the rugged steep,
    And glance around with superstitious awe :
And e'en his dog would whine, and onward creep
                With eager paw.

The withered dames, in every hamlet round,
    Strange stories of the Castle had to tell.
How big-boned skeletons had oft been found
    Down in the deep, old gloomy well ;
And how at nights there floated past, the sound
                Of ghostly knell.

Around the blacksmith's blazing forge at night,
    Such tales were told as made the flesh to creep :
And winter clothed the shattered walls in white,
    Yet none went near the grim and frowning keep ;
And rustics' teeth would chatter with affright,
                Even in their sleep.

The heart of every lad and village lass,
    Whene'er they neared the spot, with terror panted ;
And rumours spread, and so it came to pass,
    None scarce could tell, but took it all for granted,
That the fine, feudal, crumbling, tottering mass
                    Was spirit-haunted.

At length, the blushing summer 'gan her reign,
    Chasing away the wintry cold and frost ;
And birds and flow'rets followed in her train,
    And visitors and sportsmen, quite a host,
'Mong others, anatomic students, twain,
                    Who feared no ghost.

With *table-rapping* they were quite *au fait*,
    And various *spirits* answered to their rap ;
With good old "half and half" they'd "wet their clay,"
    In fact, knew all the *spirits* of the *tap*.
They "smelt a rat," and straightway vowed that they
                    Would spring the trap.

Of dread and mystery, full many a tale
    They heard, but treated them with smiles or sneers ;
And legends that had turned the rustics pale,
    Were poured in their yet unbelieving ears,
The wildest horror somehow, still would fail
                    To rouse their fears.

One stormy night, then, when the blast blew loud,
    Behold them near the dark and gloomy keep,
Nature enveloped in a misty shroud,
    On through the darkness silently they creep ;
For, see this wondrous Ghost, they both had vowed
           Ere they would sleep.

At length, above them frowns the Castle wall,
    Like some grim giant in the murky night ;
The vaulted arch now echoes their foot-fall,
    And p'raps they feel the *slightest* tinge of fright :
But now they reach the spacious gloomy hall,
           Their torch alight.

In truth, 'twas aught, but pleasant for our friends,
    Intruding thus on ghostship's recreation.
I wonder if, says one, the Ghost e'er sends
    To midnight revels, cards of invitation :
But e'en while joking, looks he backward bends,
           Of trepidation.

Now whistled shrilly o'er the hills the blast,
    And black clouds swiftly o'er the heavens sped ;
While thunder, peal on peal, came following fast,
    And levin bolts came flashing lurid red,
And Jack and Tom, their courage fading fast,
           Felt gathering dread.

'Tis midnight! see!! why do they start ?
     While each to each in mortal terror clings ;
Back flows the life blood from each throbbing heart,
     As if 'twould strain their young live's very strings!!
They see from out that gloomy crevice dart
                 Two ghost-like wings.

A something, sailing round them all in white ;
     A rustling, fluttering, through the damp chill air ;—
Two glassy eyes, superlatively bright,
     Fixing a stony fascinating glare
Of fiendish hate, and most malicious spite,
                 Full on the pair.

Is't gone ? Ah, no! again it slides,
     Like some unquiet spirit, through the gloom,
With ceaseless, noiseless fluttering, round it glides,
     A visitor from some unhallowed tomb ;
While shrieking round the walls, the tempest rides
                 On wings of doom.

Again, 'tis gone. But from a crevice in the wall
     Two orbs seem scintillating sparks of fire.
And Jack, (whom nothing long could much appall),
     Regaining courage, felt a keen desire
To probe the secret of that gloomy hall,
                 Ere they'd retire.

But all in vain, to calm Tom's fears, he tries;
　　He sooner might have calmed the Bay of Biscay—
Till handing him a flask, Tom sips and sighs,
　　And then declares it might not be *so* risky　　•
As first it seemed—such virtue lies
　　　　　　　　In good Scotch Whisky.

Still from the crevice glare those eyes of flame;
　　But Jack (whose blood was now at fever heat,
For which the whisky was, perhaps, to blame,
　　Tho' Tom's faint heart again with terror beat);
Strode forth, and Tom for very shame
　　　　　　　　Could not retreat.

Had Angelo or Rosa but been there,
　　What a wild ghastly picture they'd have painted:
Jack, pale but firm, seen by the torch's glare,
　　As if a ghostly presence ne'er had tainted
The place: Tom stretched upon a ruined stair,
　　　　　　　　For *he* had fainted.

How wildly glare those orbs of greenish hue!!
　　But Jack, now caring not for ghost, or ghoul,
Determining this midnight monster now to view,
　　Reached out his hand—then gave a dreadful howl,
As from the yawning crevice, screeching flew
　　　　　　　　A HUGE WHITE OWL!!!

This was the Ghost; but from my simple tale,
    A simple moral, if inclined, you'll mark—
Of molehills ne'er make mountains ; never quail :
    Tho' all around seems gloomy, strange, and dark,
Life's troubles are, tho' many may assail,
                        But Ghosts of Invermark.

5th September 1867.

FATHERLAND.

THE fire-flies dance beneath the shade
    Of the fragrant *Chumpa* tree,
  And the evening song of the Hindoo maid
    Comes swelling o'er the lea.
The weary sun, his radiance hides
    Behind a crimson band,
And through my Fancy now there glides
    Fond thoughts of Fatherland.

The twilight hour I loved so well,
    The fragrant heather bloom ;
The bulrush and the blue harebell,
    The golden yellow broom.
The thistle, bold ; the daisy, fair ;
    The hills so stern and grand,
Towering like giants in the air,
    The hills of Fatherland.

The little church, the tomb-stones, grey,
    Where dreary pine-trees moan ;
Where mourners come to weep and pray
    O'er loved ones, dead and gone.
The hazels, where the merry stream
    Ripples o'er golden sand ;
The northern stars that dance and gleam
    O'er dear old Fatherland.

B

I hear the distant hum of bee ;
     The lowing of the kine ;
The cushat in the holly tree,
     Where coral berries shine.
The faint, far boom of waterfall
     Deep in the forest land ;
The shepherd's shrill and cheery call
     In far off Fatherland.

The simple psalm ascending soft
     In solemn strains to God ;
The earnest, sad, imploring prayer,
     That He might ease our load.
Again, my father's voice I hear,
     Close by his side I stand,
And now come stealing on mine ear
     The songs of Fatherland.

And still, fond Fancy multiplies
     Those memories of yore ;
And visions, sweet, before me rise
     Of days that are no more.
Familiar faces smiling are,
     I stretch an eager hand ;
But grasp—a void—for, ah ! I'm far
     From friends and Fatherland.

4th September 1867.

A WISH.

From a Young Lady's Album.

IF e'er a heartfelt wish were wafted up to Heaven,—
A wish as pure as snow on upland moor that's driven ;
   A wish from out the fullness of a loving heart,
From one who oft has known sad sorrow's smart.
Then be it thine, 'tis all I have to give away—
God's blessing on thee, while upon this earth you stay.

God's blessing on thee, to preserve thee ever free
From all the griefs, and all the cares, on earth that be ;
To keep thy feet from falling, and thine eyes from tears,
And guard and guide thy footsteps through life's passing years ;
To watch that pain, or sorrow, never near thee come,
And take thee THERE, at last, to HIS eternal home.

THE CHIEFTAIN'S GRAVE.

PROUDLY swells the wailing pibroch
  O'er the heath, and down the glen ;
    And from out the frowning archway
    March a troop of stricken men :
And a pale face at the casement
  Looks with fixed and stony stare
At the sword, and dirk, and target,
  On the coffin which they bear.
*   *   *   *

Brave Macdonald ! ever foremost
  In the fierce and deadly strife ;
His trusty claymore ever gleaming
  Where the thickest blows were rife.
The grand old Chieftain, lion-hearted,
  Lifeless, lies upon the bier,
And the soul-inspiring slogan
  Ne'er again will reach his ear.
*   *   *   *

O'er the bridge, and through the bracken,
  Winding slowly round the hill ;
Through the one street of the Clachan
  Wails the solemn pibroch still.
O'er the steep and rocky pathway
  Slowly moves the funeral train,
Where the silver birch trees whisper
  In a mournful, saddened strain.

And the wild wail of the bagpipe
    Mingles with the mountain blast,
And the weird and gloomy pine-trees
    Solemn shadows o'er them cast.
Wild and haggard are those faces,
    Slow and weary is their tread ;
But each thinks of deadly vengeance,—
    Vengeance for the slaughtered dead.

But even, while the sad procession
    Reach a lone and narrow glen,
Silently are closing round them
    Fierce Red Ranald and his men.
Crouching, crawling through the heather,
    Closing slowly round their prey :
Suddenly they raise the war cry,
    Rushing down in fierce array.
But the little band of heroes
    Softly laid their burden down ;
Then each clutched his gleaming dagger ;
    While the deep, determined frown
On each brow spoke more than volumes—
    Spoke of matchless chivalry :
With their lord they oft had conquered,
    O'er his body now they'd die.
*   *   *   *

Like a rushing swollen torrent,
    Came the savage clansmen on ;

Like the blast among the pine-trees,
    When the branches bend and moan :
Like a rock in troubled ocean,
    Fiercely dashing back the spray :
Stood the stern heroic mourners,
    Like a lion brought to bay.
And the clear and ringing war cry,
    And the shriek of dying men,
And the clash of crimsoned weapons,
    Broke the silence of the glen.
Then the little phalanx wavered,
    Fighting every inch of sod ;
Yet they faced the hated foemen,
    As their souls returned to God.

*   *   *   *

Wanes the fierce unequal combat,
    Dead they lie amid the gorse ;
Till, at length, the last Macdonald
    Falls upon his Chieftain's corse :
And the base and cruel Ranald
    Left them lying where they fell ;
While the heath and quivering blue bell
    Gently tolled their funeral knell ;
And the dreary night wind rising,
    Moaned a solemn dirge-like strain ;
And the broom shook off its tassels,
    To efface the bloody stain.

*   *   *   *

Where the heath's a deeper purple,
  Where the swarthy hazels grow ;
Where, amid the whispering bracken,
  Solemn night winds softly blow.
Where the melancholy plover
  Builds her solitary nest,
There the loyal brave Macdonalds
  Round their master quietly rest.
'Neath the grey and mossy cairn,
  Where the nodding blue bells wave ;
Beside the crooning, wimpling burnie,
  There you'll find the Chieftain's grave.

4th April 1868.

THE CHITWARRAH HUNT.

WRITTEN when I first came to India, and after one of the jolliest hunts I ever enjoyed. "Old Jerusalem" was an ancient Khitmudgar. "The Burra Sahib" was our host; now, alas! dead. A truer or kinder heart never beat.

CANTO YE FIRST.

SLOWLY the morning mists arose
Above the arid plain,
   Sadly *old uncle* rubbed his nose,
Slowly and sadly donned his clothes,
And hastily awoke all those
Who deadly oath had ta'en,
That e'er the sun had reached his height,
Full many a *Geedur* dust would bite
Upon Chitwarrah plain.

By *old Jerusalem*, then, was brought
The *chota haziree*,
And hunks of beef went down each throat,
And junks of bread were set afloat
On lakes of beer and tea.
Remember 'twas in the mofussil,
Where silks and satins rarely rustle;
Where, whether wrong, or whether right,
Men rarely lose their appetite.

And so our heroes quaff'd their jorum,
And quaff'd it yet again ;
Like men who had their work before 'em,
Like honest, healthy men.

"To horse! to horse!!" is now the cry—
The dew upon the ground doth lie ;
The hounds are swift and keen ;
The fiery sun is climbing high,
And lest we should by chance get dry,
Full flasks we'll take I ween.

Up rose the *Burra Sahib* then,
And climbed upon his steed ;
Beloved by all his fellow-men,
A trusty friend indeed.
And the gaunt *Spider*, too, up rose,
Rearing his stately height ;
Noisily he blew his nose,
And angrily a kick bestows
On one unhappy wight.
Then to his prancing charger goes :
His charger milky-white.
Next, *Mangold Wurzel*, threw his legs
Across his noble bay :
Doomed is the *Geedur's* fate, who begs
Mercy of him to-day.
And *Trevor's* stately form appears
With keen and piercing eye ;

C

The divvle a bank or ditch he fears,
And as his charger snorts and rears,
The *Maori* passes by.
Across poor *Tommy's* sturdy back
His clumsy legs were thrown ;
He clutched the mane, and cried " alack ! "
With many a doleful groan.
And last of all the cavalcade
The *mysterious Fenian* came ;
With *Fiddlers'* silky mane he played ;—
The horse seemed all of angles made,
His back was sharp as razor blade ;
Yet was he fleet and game.
I ween they were six noble knights
As ever charged a foe ;
And as *Jerusalem* brought pipe lights,
They sang—" Away we go ! "
And *Prime of Life* he cursed the gout,
Because *he* couldn't go !

CANTO YE SECOND.

Now, as the shades of night retire,
The glorious beaming sun
Starts from his cloudy bed of fire,
And mounting higher, and still higher,
Tells day has now begun.
Over the course, at rapid pace,
" We prick the fiery steeds ;"

And now we near the hiding place
Of "Puss," within the reeds.
Bark dogs! Shout men! Hurrah! Hurrah!!
" Away, away!" we cry ;
Now, quick and tight the reins we draw,
With rattling hoof and eager paw,
After the hare we hie !

" Quick! quick! good horse!
" Bound o'er the course,
" Hurrah ! brave *Rover*.   On
" Yoicks ho! she's blown.
" Brave dog, well done !!
"That hare was fairly won !"
Now on again, o'er level plain
We reach the leafy brake:
Dogs, horses, men, are in again,
Our cheers, the echoes wake.
The surly *Geedur*, crouches low,
But rattling through the scrub we go ;
Then off, with many a dodge and bound,
He skims along the open ground.
But all too late, for *Rover*, bold,
Comes up, and takes tenacious hold ;
Then hounds and terriers tear and worry,
And up the panting riders hurry
To see the jackall sold.
But time would fail me quite to tell
All the adventures that befell
On that eventful day :—

How five great jackalls bit the dust;
How poor old *Fiddler* near was *bust;*
And long legged *Spider* kicked and *cussed*
As on the ground he lay.
And how *three* times (we must be brief)
The *Maori Chieftain* came to grief,
And tumbled like an autumn leaf
Over a truss of hay.

Such shouting, stamping, grinning, laughing;
Such riding, roaring, and *such* chaffing,—
One timid horse shied at a *hattie,*
And plunged his rider through a *tattie,*
Slap bang in an old hag's lap;
Who shrieking, yelled out *Bap-re-bap.*
The jackall dodging through the grass;
The braying of a *dhobee's* ass;
The hunters plying whip and spurs;
The howling of the village curs;
The Beat! the Break, the Run, the Double,
(These jackalls give a deal of trouble).
The DEATH!—The yelping, panting pack,
The whip descending with a whack,
Making the *rowdies* whine and tremble;
All formed such glorious *tout ensemble,*
That almost anything I'd give
Through such another day to live.
And then beneath the welcome shade
Of an umbrageous mango glade,

We panted, laughed, and stretched our legs,
And, fortified by sundry pegs,
Produced our pipes, and feeling chatty,
Took *otium cum dignitate.*

But soon the sun became so strong,
Our sport no more we could prolong;
And so, with laugh, and jest, and song,
Homeward we took our way.
But long the mem'ry will be kept,
How gallantly each hunter leapt
O'er nullah, ditch, and bank.
And how, at length, when all was o'er,
We paused before Chitwarrah door.—
"FIELD SPORTS" we cried, and with a roar
The noble toast was drank.

4th August 1867.

'TWAS BUT A LOCK OF HAIR.

'TWAS but a lock of hair, a tiny curly tress,
Capillae p'raps a score, p'raps more, and may be less ;
   A maiden pressed it to her lips—a being wondrous fair,
And oh! how earnestly I wished *I* were that lock of hair.

She sighed, a long vibrating sigh, 'twas really sad to hear,
And in her dark and liquid eye, I marked the pearly tear.
She spoke! and like a fairy harp, the silvery accents rung,
Or, like the cooing cadence soft, by some sweet singer sung.

"He was my idol! he, my pride ; he was my all in all ;
"And oh how joyfully he'd glance, when but his name
    I'd call !
"Together 'mong the fragrant flow'rs, from morn till eve
    we'd stray,
"And life passed like a pleasant dream upon a summer's
    day.

"Ah me! for such another, I never hope to view ;
"Thou wert so docile, gentle, kind ; so loving, faithful, true—
"But still thy image ne'er shall be erased from memory's
    log—
"My darling little Toby ; *my loving lost Lap Dog !!*

    5th December 1867.

THE "GRIFF'S REVERIE."

ALL now is hushed by the banks of the river,
  Where the whispering bamboos unceasingly quiver ;
    Save the soft murmuring ripple upon the lone bank,
Or the frogs' sullen croak 'mid the weeds, tall and dank.

How soft, sweet, and mellow, the lady moon beams ;
See how her face in the still water gleams :
She's tipping with silver each leaf of the mango,
Where the fairies are dancing a merry fandango.

How softly the solemn night's breezes are sighing,
How gently the leaves of the forest replying ;
The dew from the heavens is noiselessly falling,
The nightingale far in the covert is calling.

How cool the night air, the breezes so pleasant ;
'*Tis* India—but one almost fancies it isn't ;
Through the odorous air the fire-flies are dancing,
Like a myriad of stars in the dark foliage glancing.

Every sense is at rest—when—hark—what a bobbery !
Is it murder ? or magic, fire, fury, or robbery ?
The sounds are unearthly !—" Dear me ! what a fresh 'un !"
" You Griffin ! 'tis only a marriage procession !!"

THE ROVER'S SONG.

HURRAH! for a life on the stormy deep!
  Hurrah! for the dancing wave!
Where the gallant and true have gone to sleep,
  Far down in the mermaid's cave.
Hurrah! Hurrah!! for the whistling wind!
  Hurrah! for the roaring gale!
For the track of foam we leave behind,
  Like a ghost in the moonlight pale.

We laugh when the waves are mountains high,
  Our bark like a phantom form;
Through the wrack and the tempest on will fly,
  Hurrah! for the howling storm.
Once more, 'tis a raw and gusty day,
  Then up with the blood red flag
We sweep on our unsuspecting prey,
  Like an eagle from its crag.

Hurrah! Hurrah!! for the battle cry!
  For the gleaming sword and pike;
For the heart to battle, win or die,
  For the steady hand to strike.

Hurrah ! Hurrah !! for the bright red gold,
　　For the gems and jewels, rare ;
For the goodly spoil in our vessel's hold,
　　Which the Rover's bride shall wear.

Hurrah! Hurrah !! for the slippery deck,
　　For the shout, the curse or the prayer ;
Pull! pull away !! from the shattered wreck,
　　Heed not the yell of despair.
Fill up the wine, the blood red wine,
　　From the fields of sunny Spain ;
Drink to the storm and dashing brine,
　　We're kings of the heaving main.

Once more Hurrah ! What do we dread ?
　　What care or fear have we ?
We drown the thought of the silent dead
　　In the shout of victory.
No coffin or clod, or velvet pall,
　　Give we to the hungry wave ;
But a hammock, a flag, and a cannon ball,
　　And a cheer o'er the Rover's grave.

D

AN INTERRUPTED REVERIE.

I LOVE to muse on days that have gone by,
  (*Confound that insect, he's got in my eye*).
To call to mind the glorious deeds of old,
(*Cough, cough! why bless me! what a shocking cold!*)
To let my fancy take a backward flight
(*Plague take this horrid quill! I cannot write*).
To Rome or Athens, in their palmy days,
And wondrous visions of past glory raise.
I hear the pœans for the victory rise!
(*God bless that child! will no one stop its cries?*)
I hear the battle cry, and din of war,
I hear the thund'ring of the victor's car,
Rattling in triumph on, and by its side
I see the cohorts march in all their pride;
And citizens and priests, and many a slave,
While armour gleams, and gorgeous banners wave.
The Herald speaks, and crowds take up the cry—
"Proclaim the news! Shout! shout! for victory!!"
The cock crows—*tempus fugit*—with decorum,
I wander through the crowded forum;
I see the Emperor in his robes of state,
While proud patricians round about him wait.

The reverend Fathers, with their looks serene,
Guards, senators, plebians —motley scene !
 The arena rises up before my eyes,
I hear the gladiators' dying cries.
I hear the Nubian lion's mighty roar,
(" *Bless us ! What's that ? Confound that creaking door.*)
Through Herculaneum's palaces I roam,
' Neath marble arch, or glittering jewelled dome :
I see the cool and sparkling fountains play
O'er fairy blossoms, scattering the spray.
The air alive, with perfumes rare and rich—
(" *Hang these mosquitoes, how their bites* DO *itch ;*")
And flitting, noiseless, through the perfumed grove,
Rare forms of beauty, e'en the gods might love.
And soft notes tremble in the perfumed air,
And birds of wondrous beauty everywhere,
Like mimic rainbows flash among the trees
That bend and sway beneath the wooing breeze.
How sweet to dream away a lifetime thus !
" KHODAWUND ! KHANNA MAYS PER—BUS !!"

MY "MAIDEN SPEAR."

[Originally published in the "Oriental Sporting Magazine."]

COME, brother sportsmen, listen;
 Give an attentive ear
While I relate the story,
How I fleshed " My Maiden Spear! "
Come, all ye sporting readers
Of th' " Oriental Sporting Mag."—
I'll tell ye how I slew the boar;
Yea, killed him dead as any door,
On my gallant fact'ry nag.
Mahye was fairly over,
The weather, fine and cold;
The planters were " in clover,"
Their *cakes* were all well sold.
So four of us resolved
To kill a famous boar,
That liv'd within the sugarcane,
Close by the *moonshee's* door.
A fierce and mighty *tusker*,
For so the *chowdhry* said,
And although we'd lots of beaters,
They were very much afraid.

But we *galee kurred* and shouted,
Till we got them in a line,
To rouse the gaunt and grisly boar,
For every one amongst the four
Said, " First spear will be mine."
Then we gallopped to the corners,
And we gallopped back again ;
And we tightened up our *kummerbunds,*
And shouted to the men.
Who made such an infernal row,
The welkin rang again ;
'T would e'en have roused that famous boar
That lay in " Cosas' fen,"
Which " Aruns of Volsinium slew,"
(I know the story to be true—
Vide Macaulay's pen.)
Just then the Dangurs gave a roar
Says I to Bill—" Is that the boar?"
Says he, " I dinna ken."

   * * * *

The sugarcane is crashing,
And waving to and fro ;
The *lathee-wallahs* shouting,
As through the brake they go.
A nervous grip is on the rein,
Each spear is firmly held
The boar's afoot, that much is plain,
For every noise is quelled.

But hark that cry! *ah, bapree bap!*
Soor! soor!! A BURRA SOOR!!!
We've roused him from his morning nap,
And must his tusks secure.
Shriek—yell—crash—bang—Hurrah! Hurrah!!
He's off!!—No?—Sold again.
'Tis but a skulking *geedur*
That's taken to the plain.
A pause! What now?—He's broken back.
"Beat! Beat!! you *guddha logue!*"
We'll make him try another tack,
The crouching cunning rogue;
So in again, with shout and cry,
Might make all soordom quake;
In every nook we peer and pry,
Five anxious minutes have gone by,
Impatience gleams in every eye;
Then with a shout, away! away!!
We see our long-expected prey
Go crashing through the brake.
And faith, the chowdhry was quite right;
For see his tushes gleaming bright—
Rare tusks, and no mistake.

      *   *   *   *

With one low fierce defiant snort,
Which says, I have but this resort—
He dashes o'er the ground.
But now behind, with ringing cry,

Four hunters heel and spur do ply,
Four horses with each other vie,
With hurrying eager bound.
Four glistening spears are set in rest,
Four eager rivals are abreast ;
With fiercest ardour on we prest,
Striving to touch his flank.
"*First Spear*" cries *Jack*, but all too soon,
The shaft was wielded by a *spoon* ;
For in the ground it sank.
Next, *Bertie* raised the joyous cry.
Determined now to do or die
Three strides ; and *Bertie's* polished steel
That vigorous tusker sure must feel ;
He's but a hand's breadth from the boar.
When crash—his nag has tumbled o'er.
" Snakes !" *Bertie*, " what a spill" !
" Hurrah !" cries *Ted*, as on we flew,
" The ranks are now reduced to two,"
" That *ripper* there to kill."
Poor *Comfit*, reeled—*Ted* bounded past,
But still I floundered on,
Ted's spear was poised with steady nerve—
He aimed, but Grunter made a swerve ;
Thus *Teddy's* chance was gone.
With hope renewed, on, on I spurred,
Ne'er thinking of the risk incurred,
Till we were side by side.

His eye-balls, glaring fierce and bright ;
His tushes, gleaming iv'ry white ;
Steady a moment ; now that's right,
And then my spear, so keen and light,
Has ope'd the crimson tide—
A grunt of mingled wrath and pain.
He stands at bay with bristling mane,
His little fiery eye-balls glare
With fierce unconquerable stare.
Alas, brave Porker ! not a chance :
What boots your tusks against the lance ?
Before, behind, on every side,
Each gleaming spear, a thrust supplied.
And then, at length, when all was o'er,
We stood around the fallen boar,
And raised a ringing generous cheer,
In honor of my *Maiden Spear.*

AT NIGHT.

ALL around is dark and silent,
 Night has donned her sable veil,
 And a gloomy shadow hovers
O'er the bosom of the dale.
Cold night mists are slowly rising
From the marshy sodden soil;
And the sun has set for ever,
On another day of toil.
One more day of weary labor,
Trouble, hurry, grief, and care;
Oh, the load of wretchedness
We poor erring mortals bear!
Hurrying clouds of gloomy grandeur
Cast deep shadows as they pass;
Plain, ravine, and hill, and forest,
Merge in one confusing mass:
And sad thoughts are busy crowding
In my hot and fevered brain;
Dark and sad, like all around me,
For my heart is full of pain.
Golden dreams have fled for ever,
Smiling hopes have been represt;
And I feel an ardent longing,
"Oh, that I might be at rest."

Troubled hopes are surging through me,
Vain dumb wishes, pangs so keen ;
Dark regrets, as Fancy pictures
All the fond, "what might have been."

   *   *   *

But a rift is in the heavens,
And the stars are shining through,
Seeming like the eyes of angels,
Moist with tender pity's dew.
And a fond face smiles upon me
With a tender holy gaze—
'Tis my mother, as I saw her
In my childhood's happy days.
And a hymn, her lips had taught me,
Gently steals upon my ear ;
And a calm descends upon me,
As the hallowed strains I hear :
And I feel new life within me,
And my grief has found a balm,
And my weary heart is softened
With a holy peaceful calm.
See the moon in radiant splendour,
Flooding with her silver sheen ;
Every leaf, and nook, and crevice,
Where the gloomy shade had been.
And I pray for strength and patience,
To bear the ills that He may send ;
Hoping still, and still determined,
To do my duty to the end.

LOVE.

IKE the mysterious magnet, trembling to the pole ;
　　So is the power of Love to every ardent soul.
　　Like the quick thought the electric wire does send ;
So is the thrill of bliss fond love does lend.
Calms the toss'd heart, by rude misfortune torn,
To heavenly beauty lifts the meanest form.
Absorbs each passion, checks each wild desire,
To noble deeds and actions bids the heart aspire.
Moulds every thought, and smoothes each rugged way,
And holds o'er hearts of steel despotic sway.
Alike the greatest tyrant, and the humblest slave,
Makes brave men cowards, and makes cowards brave.
The veriest despot that the bard can sing,
Conqu'ring alike the peasant and the king.
Making a palace of the serf's abode—
An emanation from the throne of God.
Hov'ring like incense round a hallowed shrine,
My wish—ah! may *such* love be ever thine.

ALBUM EFFUSIONS.

I.

I ENVY the breeze that kisses thy cheek,
   That fondly caresses thy rich golden hair;
That hears thy sweet voice in soft, low accents speak,
   And catches thy joyous laugh thrown on the air.

I envy the flow'r that the honey bee sips,
   When 'tis gathered and placed like a gem on thy breast;
When 'tis pressed to thine arch-looking coral red lips,
   Or is placed in thy hair, like a birdling at rest.

I envy the sward where thy dainty foot treads,
   I'd kiss every leaf where a footstep had been;
The daisies with rapture are hiding their heads,
   And nod with delight 'neath the step of their queen.

I envy the peach thou hast plucked from the tree,
   The blush on thy cheek far out-rivals its bloom;
And now it's high time for a Soda and B.,
   With a quiet Manilla, alone in my room.

II.

AT the calm evening hour,
  When all things are still;
When the grey mists are stealing
  O'er valley and hill;
Faint echoes are floating
  Above the lone sea,
'Tis then I am thinking
  Of Thee—only Thee.

The cold winds are sighing
  Adown the lone vale,
And the new moon is shining,
  So ghastly and pale;
The stars, too, I fancy
  Look coldly on me,
I care not, I'm thinking
  Of Thee—only Thee.

And e'en when the stars
  Have all vanished from sight,
And the heavens are shrouded
  In darkness and night;
What a heavenly radiance
  My heart *still* would see,
If I knew that You sometimes
  Were thinking of *me.*

III.

JEANNIE'S BLUE E'E.

OH, bright are the gems on a queen's snowy brow,
    And sweet are the flow'rs that on mossy banks grow;
    But brighter by far, and sweeter to me,
    Is the kind couthie glance o' my Jeannie's blue e'e.

As some beaming star in heaven's blue dome
Kindly lights up the pilgrim's weary way home,
So my heart's lighted up, and my steps bound with glee,
When I feel the kind glance o' my Jeannie's blue e'e.

When I'm weary and worn, despairing and sad,
What is't lights my eye? makes my brow clear and glad?
Makes my heart bound with joy, gay, gladsome, and free?
'Tis the sweet winning glance o' my Jeannie's blue e'e.

She's fairer to me than the sweetest wee flow'r
That e'er bloom'd in beauty, on bank, or in bow'r;
Oh, to gain but her love! I could lay down and dee
For one tender glance o' her bonnie blue e'e.

Give the miser his gold, and the warrior fame,
The friendless a friend, and the nameless a name,
The mean raise to greatness; but, oh! give to me;
Only one loving glance o' my Jeannie's blue e'e.

May her brow aye be clear, and her glance ever bright,
Her bosom aye happy, her heart ever light ;
May sorrow and care, far, far from her flee ;
May a tear never dim her bonnie blue e'e.

And when her sun sets on that glorious shore,
Where parting, and sorrow, and sin, are no more—
With my whole soul I pray, that the last glance may be
A glance full of peace in my Jeannie's blue e'e.

IV.

On seeing a rather gushing effusion about living on a lonely isle in an atmos-
phere of light, love, and general lunacy.

IT'S all very well for a poet
   To sing about "some lonely isle,"
"Like a gem in the ocean ;" but blow it !
   'Twould only be nice for a while.

At first, it *might* be rather jolly
   To live all alone in a cave
Embowered in ivy and holly,
   And "lulled by the murmuring wave."

With a pipe and a *peg* you *might* do it,
   For a week you might live like a lord ;
But then your beer, who is to brew it ?
   And pipes on "lone isles" are'nt stored.

With a gun fowling-piece or good rifle
    A very nice fortnight you'd spend ;
Caps and powder, of course, are a trifle,
    But for them where are you to send ?

Then the flies and mosquitoes would bite you,
    And curtains, of course, you havn't got;
And wouldn't wild *janwars* delight you,
    When you hadn't got powder and shot !

No, no ! it may look well on paper,
    But try it, and soon you would see
How its beauty would " pass like a vapour,"
    So none of your " lone isles" for me.

Give me but a snug little cottage,
    With a dear little wife by my side,
And the poets may have all the islands
    That ever were laved by the tide.

THE "WALL-FLOWER'S" LAMENT.

'VE paced your "academic halls," and many a prize have got,
And now I'm very snug, and yet mine a'int a happy lot.
 The reason, girls, you'd never guess, not if you'd every chance;
Then listen, while I tell you—'Tis because *I cannot dance.*

I've fallen in love with scores of girls, but what's the earthly use?
They see me in the ball-room stand, a solitary goose.
I fetch refreshments, strive to please, but after each advance,
Some smirking dandy takes my place, because I cannot dance.

With one fair belle, the other night, I made the running strong—
I whispered, chatted, laughed and talked, both fluently and long;
I watched her eyes, I would have bled, for only one kind glance:
But no! she looked the other way; she knew I couldn't dance.

I tried another—all went well—she looked amused and pleased,
When up comes Mr. Percy Jones, from supper-room released.
She took his arm.   I scowled, and 'saw them round the ball-room
 prance,
But I had to grin and bear it; for you know I cannot dance.

At length, in desperation, I asked a lady's hand
For one quadrille, although I knew not where to take my stand:
I tore her dress, trod on her toes: her eyes flashed like a lance,
As she said with cruel irony—"How *very* well you dance."

So you see I'm most unhappy, and I often heave a sigh,
But sighing *isn't* dancing, and the girls all pass me by.
I'm neither rich nor handsome, and I fear my only chance
Is to wait for some one like myself, who never learned to dance.

                                                                F

BONNIE MORN.

Written for the O. S. M., on the occasion of the death of a favourite
hunter belonging to J. M'L——Esq., killed at Peeprah while pig-sticking.

ALAS! my "Brave Bonnie," the pride of my heart,
The moment has come when from thee I must part : ·
No more wilt thou hark to the hunter's glad horn,
My brave little Arab, my poor " Bonnie Morn."

How proudly you bore me at bright break of day ;
How gallantly "led" when the boar "broke away ;"
But no more, alas ! thou the hunt shall adorn,
For here he lies dying, my dear " Bonnie Morn."

He'd neigh with delight when I'd enter his stall,
And canter up gladly on hearing my call :
Rub his head on my shoulder while munching his corn,
My dear gentle Arab, my poor " Bonnie Morn."

Or out in the grass, when a pig was in view,
None so eager to start, when he heard a " halloo ;"
Off, off, like a flash, the ground spurning with scorn ;
He aye led the van, did my brave " Bonnie Morn."

O'er nullah and ditch, o'er hedge, fence, and bank,
No matter ! *he'd* clear it, aye in the front rank ;
A brave little hunter as ever was born,
Was my grand Arab fav'rite, my good " Bonnie Morn."

Or when in the "ranks," who so steady and still,
None better than " Bonnie," more " up" in his drill.
His fine head erect, eyes flashing with scorn,
Right fit for a charger was staunch " Bonnie Morn."

And then on the "course," who so willing and true ?
Past the " stand," like an arrow the Bonnie horse flew.
No spur his good rider need ever have worn,
For he aye did his best, did my fleet " Bonnie Morn."

And now here he lies, the good little horse,
No more he'll career in the hunt or the " course."
My heart it is weary, I feel quite forlorn ;
I *can't* help a tear, 'tis for poor " Bonnie Morn."

Ah ! blame not my grief, for 'tis deep and sincere,
As a friend and companion I held " Bonnie" dear.
No true sportsman ever such feelings will scorn,
As I heave a deep sigh for my steed, " Bonnie Morn."

And even, in death, when in anguish he lay,
When his life's blood was drip—dripping—slowly away,
His last thought was still of the master he'd borne,
He neighed, licked my hand, and thus died " Bonnie Morn."

PROVERBIAL PHILOSOPHY.

After Tupper—A long way.

WHEN "down on your luck," and gloomy with care,
 When the heart's heavy burden you scarcely can bear ;
 When the footstep is dull, and the merry laugh hushed,
Fond hopes unrealized, blighted or crushed.
Frowned at by fortune, deserted by friends ;
When not even *one* eye a kindly glance lends.
" *Nil desperandum*"—away with repining,
" *For every cloud has its silver lining.*"
When some former flatterer passes you by,
A sneer on his lip, and contempt in his eye ;
Or some "jack in office," with more head than brains,
A lackey-sent answer to your appeal deigns.
Still stick to your manhood, ne'er flatter or fawn,
" *For the darkest hour is before the dawn.*"
Fear not and fret not, set fortune at bay,
And remember " *that every dog has his day.*"
Be manly and dignified, steady and strong,
Ne'er halt on your way, though the path may be long.
There oft may be worry, vexation, heart-burning ;
But " *even the longest lane has a turning.*"
Let each aim be lofty, and each action just,
In Virtue and Providence put ye your trust ;
Then frowning Dame Fortune will soon change her mood,
" *For 'tis an ill wind that blows nobody good.*"

SONGS.

THINGS I HAVE SEEN.

Air.—" Cheer up Sam."

COME, listen to my ditty, I'll tell you what I've seen,
 Since first I came to Hindostan, a griffin rather
 green.
I've seen great alterations, oppressions too, and sins;
And it strikes me that it isn't aye, the better nag that wins.

Chorus.—
 But cheer up boys, and don't let your spirits go down,
 Don't fear, but in the " straight run home," the white will
 beat the brown.

I've seen a native give *salaam,* and show one some respect;
But *salaams* are things that now-a-days we really don't
 expect.
" Good mo'ning, sahib.—Dam you r'ics," is what they glibly
 say ;
" I'bery learned Hindoo Sah—I Government B. A —!! "

Chorus.—
 But cheer up boys, and don't let your spirits go down, &c.

I've seen a great commander prosecute his aide-de-camp,
Because he found the tally of his jams and pickles wrong ;

But such sharp economics one scarce can wonder at,
When "rugged Jan" himself still sticks to his worn out
coat and hat.

Chorus.—
But cheer up boys, and don't let your spirits go down, &c.

I've seen a Government, whose aim was just, and kind, and
plain :
Up with the native and down with us, they cried with might
and main.
No magistrate to a planter's house to dine must ever go ;
If he does, he'll lose promotion and be sent to Jericho.

Chorus.—
But cheer up boys, and don't let your spirits go down, &c.

I've seen our well-tilled factory lands, by force illegal sown ;
But the magistrates they didn't care, but left it quite alone.
If you tried expostulation, whene'er you turned your back,
The *lathees* whistled round your head, with many a sounding
whack.

Chorus.—
But cheer up boys, and don't let your spirits go down, &c.

If to the thanna you complained, a native heard you there ;
If to the court, a native filled the magisterial chair.   [case—
No matter tho' you'd been half killed, he'd still dismiss the
Cause why ?—They one and all belonged to the gentle
Hindoo race.*

Chorus.—
But cheer up boys, and don't let your spirits go down, &c.

---

* *Note.*—This is an allusion to cases that were dismissed by the moonsifs
and native deputies.

Now, if a native's only charged with any serious crime,
Do all you can to let *him* off, at most with a simple fine.
But the white man must be sent to jail, for that's the modern
　mode
In which our magistrates now-a-days read " The Indian Penal
　Code."

Chorus.—
　But cheer up boys, and don't let your spirits go down, &c.

Yet there was a time when an English arm was worth its
　weight in gold ;
But although we saved the country then, we're now left out
　in the cold.
The high places in the synagogues are now to the heathen
　given ;
So the Christian may go to blazes, while the nigger goes
　straight to Heaven.

Chorus.—
　But cheer up boys, and don't let your spirits go down, &c.

THE INCOME TAX OF 1870.

Air.—"Tramp, Tramp."

WHILE Bobbie Lowe at home is doing all he can,
    Taking loads from off the tax-payers' backs;
    Out here Dicky Temple's taking quite another
        plan,
And preaching up an odious Income Tax.
Chorus.—

        So pay, pay, pay and be contented,
        Though the hard gripe of poverty you feel;
        And 'tis likely by-and-by some other tax he'll
          try,
        When time one more *deficit* shall reveal.

There's that mysterious lot, the "Public Waste Depart-
    ment,"
Have been going on in such a reckless way,
That of useless bridges, barracks, jobs, they've now such an
    assortment,
    That through the nose we're having now to pay.
Chorus.—So pay, pay, pay and be contented, &c.

Our roads are a disgrace; no ferry boats we've got;
    Though a lakh or two we yearly have to raise;
But a poor mofussil district, of course, may "go to pot,"
    While for Simla or Calcutta roads it pays.*
    Chorus.—So pay, pay, pay and be contented, &c.

Note.—Since this was written the local funds are now spent on local roads.

We are honest Englishmen, don't care to scheme and lie,
 So we fill our "income schedule," full and fair;
But our neighbour, the "mahajun," his name—say Kassee
 Rai,
 Pays but ten "*dibs*," though he has a lakh to spare.

 Chorus.—So pay, pay, pay and be contented, &c.

If the assessor has a doubt, and would want a little more,
 He's only got to wink and hold his hand,
In which palm oil is dropped, though Kassee's heart is sore,
 But then he's quick a hint to understand.

 Chorus.—So pay, pay, pay and be contented, &c.

Of course it's soon made good; for the ryots cannot pay,
 So they come to Kassee for a trifling loan,
Which is charged at cent per cent., though the ryots know
 and say,
 Their mahajun has a pulseless heart of stone.

 Chorus.—So pay, pay, pay and be contented, &c.

If your evil luck be such, that you're in Government
 employ,
 Your case is then of every hope bereft;
Your "*tullub*" first they cut, then with most sarcastic joy
 They hand you o'er the balance which is left.

 Chorus.—So pay, pay, pay and be contented, &c.

With the Council now at home legislation's but a farce;
 No wonder though our enemies should smile,

A nod is but required to make any nonsense pass,
    For the Emperor of India is " Argyll."

    Chorus.—So pay, pay, pay and be contented, &c.

Till we're fairly represented, this injustice will increase,
    For every booby who may dabble in finance ;
Though India with one voice may call on him to cease ;
    Yet, fearless, on his hobby horse he'll prance.

    Chorus.—So pay, pay, pay and be contented, &c.

Let all India then unite, pull together heart and hand,
    Cast vain rivalry and jealousy aside.
Let the people's voice be heard, a useless council quick
    disband,
Let's appoint our men our own affairs to guide.

        Chorus.—Then we'll pay, pay, pay and be con-
        tented,
        And no more injustice will we feel.
        If you give us but a share in managing our own
        affairs,
        Why, we'll gladly put our shoulders to the wheel.

WEARIN' O' THE GREEN.

A Parody : written about the time when the great Fenian excitement
was making such a stir at home, and shortly after the Duke of Edinburgh
was fired at and wounded in Sydney.

CII Paddy dear, and did yez hear the news that's goin,
    roun'—
    The Fenians they are springin' up loike mushrooms
    from the groun';
No more St. Pathric in his grave will shleep and be at rest,
These dirty Yankee Fenians are becomin' such a pest.
I would loike to take a dozen of them, firmly by the hand ;
What my opinion of them is, they soon would undherstand.
They're the biggest dirty cowards that ivver yet were seen—
Blowin' up the jail of Clerkenwell loike a powdher magazine.

I think the colour they should wear, should be the devil's
    black ;
If e'er they're shot in battle, shure it will be in the back.
Then take a good strong hempen rope, and hang them in a
    row,
For such mean murtherin villains are not worth the name of
    foe
When laws allow a scoundhrel to do all the ill he can,
And whin robbery and murther are no longer undher ban,
Thin perhaps a Fenian's dirty face amongst us may be seen ;
But till that toime the devil take the Wearin' o' the Green.

Loike thistle down upon the air, conspiracy has spread :
No man in England now is safe to lie down in his bed.
Our gallant prince, beloved by all, they basely tried to slay,
But Heaven stretched forth a saving hand, and turned the
    ball away.
May curses rest upon the heads of all the coward crew,
May speedy vengeance dog their steps and retribution true.
Down, down with every rebel spawn that wears the rebel
    green,
While every loyal Briton cries, " God bless our noble Queen."

I KNEW I MUST BE DREAMING.

Written during the Franco-German War, and published in the O.S.M.

THE other night, in pensive mood, I sat beside my fire,
  Watching the flames leap up and glow, and flicker
  and expire.
The papers talked of war and strife, and pestilence and pain,
And I slumbered till my dreams were filled with visions of
  the slain.
I thought I saw them start to life, in myriads onwards
  streaming,
And I thought there was an end of strife—what a pity, 'twas
  but dreaming.

And still I slept, while many a dream came flitting o'er my
  brain,
Which, if you'll kindly listen now, I'll tell to you again.
As in all dreams, of course, you know the visions were
  confused,
For now they saddened, now perplexed, and now again
  amused.
I thought I'd got a "management," my rats with produce
  streaming ;
But I'd to go and count the coolies, and I knew I must be
  dreaming.

I thought Calcutta tradesmen, and Messrs. Jones and Co.,
Put a fair price on their goods ; in fact, a price I thought
quite low.
Though far into a foreign land to earn my bread I'd come,
I thought things weren't *half* so dear as what they were at
home.
I thought I'd quick my fortune make, how to spend it I
was scheming,
When the dâkman brought my yearly bills, and I knew I
had been dreaming.

I thought Bengalee Baboos were modest, when they talked,
And cricket played, and foot-ball too, and for big wagers
walked.
That " Griffs" grim tigers slew each day, and forty-inch
" tuskers" speared,
And swore in Anglo-Hindostanee by Mahomed's beard,
At least that was in their letters home, I could not mistake
the meaning,
And, of course, I thought " 'twas all serene," till I found
I'd just been dreaming.

I thought I met a " *khansamah*," who never stole the tea,
And a " *bearer*" who would serve your friend, yet never ask a
fee ;
A " *chowkeedar*," who never slept, was *always* to be seen,
And a *syce* who always fed his horse, and kept the harness clean.
A faithful set of slaves in fact, with honest faces beaming,
But my tea still goes, and I lose my clothes, and I know
I must be dreaming.

I thought I met a native, who would never tell a lie,
And to shirk his fair amount of work would never, never try.
Who had a soul above a bribe, an ear for music too,
And who used his fists like an Englishman, and away his
"*lathee*" threw.
Who *always* greased his "*hackree*" wheels, to prevent their
horrid screaming,
And who never screwed his bullocks' tail, but I know I must
be dreaming.

I thought those fragrant college youths, with B. A. to their
name,
Were capable of blushing, and knew the sense of shame ;
That "Young Bengal," with loyal gratitude, in fact did burn,
And didn't 'gainst the hand that fed them, like a cobra turn.
That the native press, with loyal thoughts and sentiments, was
teeming,
And stamped down maudlin, scurrilous froth, but I *know*
I MUST be dreaming.

I thought I met a planter, who never talked of "*shop*,"
Nor drivelled aye about his lands, his produce, and his crop ;
Nor criticised his neighbours' fields, nor punched his bearer's
head,
And never even grumbled when his "income tax" he paid.
Who never 'gainst some native swell, for a good long lease was
scheming,
And who *always* paid his assistants WELL, but I KNOW I MUST
BE DREAMING.

I thought I saw a STATION, where THE LADIES, all agreed ;
To idle stories and reports, gave not the slightest heed ;
Where curious tongues were silent; and *scandal* never came
To taint each generous action, with the shadow of its shame.
Where men could lead a happy life, each household always
    deeming
It best to mind their own affairs, but I KNOW I MUST BE
    DREAMING.

I thought that TRUTH AND HONOR were the guiding rules of
    life—
Peace reigned on earth, away had flown all envy, hate, and
    strife ;
That each man loved his neighbour, and battled 'gainst THE
    WRONG,
And Faith, and Love, and Liberty, waxed beautiful and strong.
And I thought how bright, and fair, and true, this world of love
    was seeming,
Then strive and pray for this glad time, and an end to all
    false dreaming.

THE PLANTER'S BUNGALOW.

Air.—" The Jolly Waggoners."

" H! the Pope, he leads a happy life,"
　　At least so says the song ;
　But we, planters, lead a happier,
Sure you don't think me wrong ?
With our races, sports, and hunting,
　　And a jolly bungalow.

　　　　Chorus.—Sing hi my lads, sing ho ;
　　　　　　　　Drive on my lads, hi oh—
　　　　　　　　Who wouldn't spend his days
　　　　　　　　In a planter's bungalow ?

When the days are fine and cold, my boys,
　We have a hunting meet ;
Where we scour across the plain
　On our chargers, strong and fleet ;
Or crashing through the jungle
　　We spear our grisly foe.

　　　　Chorus.—Sing hi my lads, sing ho, &c.

When mounted on our hockey " *tats*,"
　We drive along the ball,
And we're quickly up and on again ;
　If o'er we got a fall ;
To baulk a run, or win a goal,
　　Like a torrent on we go.

　　　　Chorus.—Sing hi my lads, sing ho, &c.

Upon the *vats*, in summer time,
　We toil, and fag, and fret;
Even then our situation
　We never can regret—
Beneath the punkah in the house
　The fragrant weed we blow.

　　　Chorus.—Sing hi my lads, sing ho, &c.

But when " *Mahye* " is fairly o'er,
　The " *cakes* " all packed away,
Hurrah then for a planter's life!
　We're happy night and day;
With races, balls, and social " meets,"
　All sorts of sport we show.

　　　Chorus.—Sing hi my lads, sing ho, &c.

Hark to the music of the pack,
　As through the brake they wind,
A dodging doubling fox ahead,
　And dear old PAT behind.
Whoop! Tally ho!! the brush is won,
　YOUNG PAT the horn doth blow.

　　　Chorus.—Sing hi my lads, sing ho, &c.

'Tis glorious, from the racing stand,
　To see some fav'rite horse,

Like DELPHOS, PAT, or VETERAN,
  Careering o'er the course,
For the planter's nags and colours
  To the front not seldom show.

> *Chorus.*—Sing hi my lads, sing ho, &c.

When " estimates" are on the board,
  And the money market " stiff,"
We run down to Calcutta
  And with "the Agents" tiff—
At old MORAN's or THOMAS',
  Or Begg Dunlops & Co.

> *Chorus.*—Sing hi my lads, sing ho, &c.

And even when we're very "*greeb*,"
  "*Cooch purwah rukta nahin*;"—
To the "*Manager*," "come tip the dibs,"
  Is all we've got to say.
If stores run short, we write to "*Jones*,"
  Or "Bishnauth Law & Co."

> *Chorus.*—Sing hi my lads, sing ho, &c.

We try to act like honest men,
  Although we've been decried ;
Your autocrats don't know us well,
  Because they've never tried.
We're LOYAL, and we may be led,
  But never "*druv*" you know.

> *Chorus*—Sing hi my lads, sing ho, &c.

Then let us pull together boys,
   Drown envy, care and strife ;
I pledge each brother planter,
   And each brother planter's wife,
For the dearest, sweetest, DEST of all,
   Are the ladies as we know.
      One pledge then e'er we go,
        Let the brimming bumper flow,
      And may happiness aye dwell
        In each " PLANTER'S BUNGALOW."

THE NEW FURLOUGH RULES.

This was written at the request of a "Junior Civilian" in 1868, and though the rules were afterwards much modified, still the song pretty accurately states what *at first* was really projected.—

'TWAS just the other day (at least, so "the papers" say,)
The "seniors" held a private consultation,
- To see how they could best, feather each his cosy nest
Without letting down, of course, their reputation.
Oh my! how their faces shone,
As they thought with an air of exultation,
That they would eat the peach; while the "juniors" sucked
the stone—
What a gen'rous piece of ratiocination!!

> *Chorus.*—Oh my! look upon them now,
> Just take a quiet observation;
> If they pass the "Furlough Rules," won't the
> juniors look like fools?
> Even now they're in a state of agitation.

" The first thing to be done," quoth the 'seniors,' every one,—
" Is this devoutly wished for consummation?"
" Every two or three years or so, to England we must go,
" Yet still retain our well-paid situations.

" Of course, we're all agreed—lots of money we will need ;
" For London is a most expensive 'station.'
" And so, while we're away, we propose to draw half pay"—
Motion carried with a deal of acclamation.

 Chorus.—Oh my ! look upon them now, &c.

" What matter, though for years 'mid struggling hopes and
" A 'junior' to his work has shown devotion ;   [fears,
" Mid worry and turmoil, 'mid sickness, care, and toil,
" Who cares ? We cannot let him have promotion.
" *Our* work, while *we're* away, he will do but ; all the pay
" We will draw without the slightest hesitation ;
'· And as soon as we come back, why then, of course, we'll pack
" Him off again to some mofussil station.

 Chorus —Oh my ! look upon them now, &c.

" We're, of course, a favoured class ; so if the rules but pass,
" When our term of service gains its termination,
" We'll retain our lordly wealth, fame, luxuries, and health,
" In the *hills* or England spend a nice vacation.
" But the kernel of the scheme—in fact, the very cream
" Of the joke, is the gentle moderation,
" We to the juniors show, saying—" Boys, before we go,
" *You'll* provide the funds for all our recreation,

 Chorus.—Oh my ! look upon them now, &c.

   (Indignant Junior log.)

" Yes, while those *already* rich, lordly dwellers in " the ditch,"
" Will enjoy themselves in ease and relaxation :

" What remotest chance have we, home and friends again to see,
" Gainst fever, liver, heat, and irritation ;
" While the ' seniors' trot about, to opera and rout,
" We must fag, and fret, and toil in close cutcherry :
" And it surely won't improve the temper of our love
" To know 'tis with our *tullop* they make merry.

  Chorus.—Oh my ! look upon them now, &c.

" But this ' kettle of nice fish,' isn't yet upon the dish,
" And the scheme may turn out yet but an abortion :
" Indeed, one scarce believes, e'en a gang of arrant thieves
" Could have the face to make such an extortion.
" ' A bird in hand at best,' ' is worth,' you know, the rest ;
" So ' juniors,' let us form a combination !
" Ours is no vulgar rant—fair play is all we want,
" Not a set of rules to work our degradation."

  Oh my ! Action is the cry !
  Away with doubt and every hesitation.
  " While the sun shines, make your hay" " Work while
   it is to-day,"
  Or you'll soon be in a state of "*botheration.*"

THE RIFLE, THE ROD, AND THE SPEAR.

COME, brothers, now join me in fancy recalling ;
  A few of those scenes that we all love so well ;
    And while the grey shades of the twilight are falling,
    On passed happy days'let our memories dwell.
Ah ! smooth was our brow, and our step then was lighter :
Our wan leaf is now somewhat withered and sere,
Yet our pulses get stirred, and our dulled eye grows brighter ;
And the grasp on our old comrade's hand will grow tighter
At the toast of " the Rifle, the Rod, and the Spear."

D'you mind that lone reach, where the river was sweeping
In swift silvery billows down to the far sea ;
Where the birch and the fern pearly dew drops were weeping,
And the primrose was wooed by the murmuring bee.
Across the blue heavens a few clouds are sailing,
The swish of a " *cast*" now sounds sharp on your ear ;
Your " *fly*" on the bright silver stream is now trailing—
Quick ! strike ! a six-pounder !! You can't help a cheer.
And you cry as his golden scales gleam in the sunshine.—
Hurrah for the Rifle, the Rod, and the Spear.

Do you mind when we met on the braes there together ;
In life's golden prime, when we knew not a care ;
And our glad, cheery voices, rang over the heather,
As we brought down a moorcock or "spotted" a hare.
The bleating of far distant sheep in the valley,
The laverock's song in the heavens so clear ;
The rich, hearty laugh at each humorous sally,
The absence of care and the freedom from fear :
You may rave of your opera, dote on your ballet!
But give ME the Rifle, the Rod, and the Spear.

Far up the dark glen, where the mountain mists gather,
And the frowning crags take each a weird gloomy form ;
Where the " Unich"* foams over its grey bed of granite,
And the scream of the eagle is heard o'er the storm.
D'ye mind that grey boulder ? You lay down upon it
The reward of your patience and toil drawing near
One second—old Hugh puts his hand to his bonnet,
Fast speeds the sure bullet, and down comes your deer ;
'Tis the grandest old head in the forest you've won it.
Hurrah for the Rifle, the Rod, and the Spear !

Or do you remember those three years of " cram—"
Conic sections, dead languages, " Euclid" and " Forbes :"
The nights spent in dreams of that dreaded " *Exam* ; "
The days spent in grinding irregular verbs.
What cheered up your gloom and gave nerve to your system.

---

* Unich, a stream in Forfarshire.

I

What quickened your pulses and banished your fear ?
'Twas tho thought—when you'd passed, how you'd rattle
     and twist'em.
Those tigers and pigs in *this* hot hemisphere,
And your constant key-note, in the P. and O. boat;
Was hurrah for the Rifle, the Rod, and the Spear.

Do you mind your lone watch in that dense bit of jungle,
The huge fiery sun beating down on your head,
The half-expressed fear you might after all bungle,
And instead of the slayer, be slain instead?
Not one breath of air stirs the vast stretch around you,
But the yells of the beaters are now drawing near.
A rustling—you tremble. At length HE has found you
Face to face for a moment, then twenty feet clear
He leaps—for your bullet has crashed through his forehead.
Hurrah for the Rifle, the Rod, and the Spear!

D'ye remember that glorious day in the " *Jowah*" ?
Ah well you remember: your poor little horse
So gashed, that you buried him under the " *Mhowah*,"
And dropped a warm tear o'er his quivering corse.—
Yes, w'ant he a tusker—a " one'er" to charge—
That noble old boar that we killed by the mere,
With tushes like daggers, a hide like a targe,
And a grand fighting heart that had *never* known fear.
Then at night how we cheered, when our generous host
Gave the toast of the Rifle, the Rod, and the Spear.

Well, pleasures are fleeting, full many are vain,
But the Rifle, the Rod, and the Spear, stand the test ;
You may throw them aside, but again and again
You'll return to them still with an ever new zest.
And whether at home, or on India's hot strand,
Be your game, the bright salmon or huge mahaseer :
Do you follow your quarry by water or land,
Be it boar, bear or tiger, or moorcock or deer ;
You'll still drink my toast, let each true sportsman pledge me.
Hurrah for the Rifle, the Rod, and the Spear !

NOT FOR ME.

 GAZE in her eyes, and a dreamy look,
Half sweet, half sad, I see;
Like a veiled sunbeam in a forest nook,
But that look is not for me.

On her face a radiant dimpling smile,
Like the sheen on sun-lit sea;
But my yearning heart may break the while,
For her smile is not for me.

I hear her whisper, soft and low,
What pleasant tones they be;
But there's no responsive look or sigh,
No whisper soft for me.

And looks, and smiles, and tender words,
She scatters far and free;
But that one word I long to hear—
That—" *yes*"—is not for me.

What matter, she's mine idol still,
And wishes, sure are free;
I pray still for *her* happiness,
Though joy is not for me.

HINTS.

OULD you learn to be popular,
 Then well your neighbour scan ;
 Find out every fault and foible,
 And the flames of folly fan.
Confidential talk invite,
Then retail it high and low ;
And you're sure to be most popular,
As things at present go.

Would you learn to be witty,
Pilfer sayings, old and new ;
If a joke is ever uttered,
Say it once belonged to you.
Be rude, unkind, and vulgar,
'Neath the guise of "speaking truth ;"
And from downright honest terror,
You'll be called a witty youth.

Would you wish to be " *most courteous ?*"
Wear a false and hackneyed smile ;
Fawn and flatter whom you hate,
Though your heart o'erflows with bile.
If the truth should be unpleasant,
Tell a genteel, modest lie ;
And you're sure to get the credit
For the height of courtesy.

Would you learn to be wealthy ?
Just look around and find
How worth gives place to roguery,
Low cunning stands for mind.
How vulgar ostentation,
And meretricious show,
Swamps good old-fashioned honesty,
And TRUTH is voted " *slow.*"

Do you want a name for wisdom?
Get the gossip of the town ;
If a rival wants to argue,
Just glibly talk him down.
Be coarse and contradictory ;
Insist that *you* know best ;
For loud assertion now-a-days
Of wisdom is the test.

Would you learn to be HAPPY ?
Consult your neighbour's case ;
Without deceit or flattery
Strive simply how to please.
With kindly deeds of sympathy
Thy brother's pathway strew,
And in making OTHERS happy thus,
Why, thou'lt be happy too.

THE RAJGHAT PARTY.

Written for the O. S. M.

'TIS but a lay of the same old thing,
   The brave old sport of yore,
   Of all field sports the noblest,
The slaying of the boar.
When he rushes through the covert,
As the hunters press him sore ;
Till he stands at bay,
In the grand old way,
We have seen so oft before.

No gentle puny sport I ween,
For a perfumed dainty " *swell* ;"
But an eye that's quick, and true, and keen,
And a wrist (*you* know the kind I mean,)
And a boy that some good sport has seen,
Are the characters that tell.

And thus I quietly pondered,
As I looked on the good array ;
Nine riders bold, all good men told,
At Rajghát the other day.

Our *host*, in sporting circles famed,
Was eager for the fray !
" *Commissioner Bump*," and *Price* that " trump,"
And the " *Butcha*," " *Ted*," and " *Bob*," in a lump,"
Came quickly on their way :
Behind came " *Hammy*," and our friend the " Lammie,"
And the writer of this lay.

The sky was flecked with cloudlets, grey,
Quick changing into gold ;
A soft mist on the jungle lay,
Through which, dull loomed the orb of day,
Across the level wold.
Like some weird, dark, mysterious line,
Three hundred beaters stood,
Their dusky forms limned, sharp and fine,
Against the bosky wood.

Not a breath of air was stirring,
As the beating it began ;
But our merry jokes and laughter
Along the valley ran.
' Twas a likely piece of jungle,
We were sure to get a " *find*,"
And we'd rather stay
The live-long day,
Than leave one boar behind.

And now the din is rising
Into the startled air,
The savage boar apprising,
That he'd better quit his lair:
A partridge gets up, whirring
Over the waving reeds,
And each sportsman's blood is stirring,
As through his veins it speeds:
We are settling in our saddles,
And we grasp and poise the spear,
And each gets placed, for the coming race,
For we know the boar is near.

A sudden waving in the grass!
" *Kya kurta Jemadar?*"
" *Ah bap-re-bap! Soor! burra Soor!!!*"
" *Here Baithe! khubberdar!!*"
Bah! it's a sow—with sudden bound
She crashes through the brake,
And off, like huntsman after hound,
L——follows in her wake:
" Divvle a spear he'll get," says *Ted*,
" Nor even save his stake."
We watched the trio disappear,
Horse, L——, and grunting sow,
And we could'nt help laughing,
As we thought of the chaffing,
Poor L—— was in for now.

K

"A stern old tusker's broken back!!!"
Five sportsmen hurry round,
And closely follow on his track,
Across the open ground.
"I pity that pig, " quoth " *Teddy—*"
"He's a ' dead un,' I'll be bound."

"Look out! LOOK OUT!" cries *Hammy*,
"There's a dozen on a head,"
And away they go
In a goodly row,
Ere the words were scarcely said.
We hold back for a moment,
To let them clear the brake ;
Then away we hie with a ringing cry,
As we give the reins a shake :
"Finishing all the way, by Jove!"
'Twas a spurt, and no mistake.
Foremost on course or open field,
Brave *Jamie* led the way,
Hammy and I came on behind,
Spurring the brown and grey.
But another fate was left for us,
(Ah! woe the luckless day,)
In a nasty hole, we both did roll,
And our horses broke away.

When we found no bones were broken,
We soon got up again ;

What we said, I'll leave unspoken,
For 'twas less polite than plain:
'Twas no use crying o'er spilt milk,
For already the boar was slain.

But now our star of fortune shone,
(Our wand'ring steeds regained ;)
Ere but a short half hour had gone,
Three boars our spears had stained:
And far across the valley,
We heard a distant shout,
Proclaiming a fresh victory,
Another pig "rubbed out."
And now the girths we slacken,
To give the nags a blow ;
We have a peg and a little "snack,"
Reform the beaters on the track,
Then on again we go.

What a splendid sight, on a sunny day,
'Tis to see the waving line,—
Spears glinting, branches crashing,
And when we get a "SIGN."
What a sudden wavering motion,
As the beaters hurry back ;
How they yell and shout, as the old *mâhout*
Puts the *hâthi* on the track.
And round the corner of the scrub,
A bristly mass uprears ;

Gives a surly look, and an angry snort,
As he slowly disappears.
See on ahead! by that Kaira bush
A rustling in the grass,
He's going, boys!—BEAT! JEMADAR!!
We can't let this one pass.
Keep back, *Ted! Butcha* DO hold hard!!
STEADY BOYS—LET HIM GO!
Away! away!! Let the "Làtchfords" play;
By Jove, he's a noble foe.
He looks like a regular Tartar,
'Tis a grand and a thrilling race;
For a full mile and a quarter
We went at racing pace.
The wind goes rushing past us,
We madly work the rein,
But he's reached the *nullah* on ahead,
We're this time "SOLD AGAIN."

He's lying in the water,
In a dense and tangled lair,
With blood-shot eyes and heaving flanks,
But yet he'll not despair.
His heart's a brave and stout one,
And when he can no more,
With defiant grunt,
He'll STILL show front,
Though dripping red with gore,
And bravely die without one cry,
Like a grand old grisly boar.

He's off again, but slowly—
His mind's made up to fight.
But now behind. *Brown Duchess*
Comes up like streak of light!
The FIRST SPEAR's pierced the tawny hide—
That cruel spear so bright ;
Now filmy with the hot life's blood,
Dear to a sportsman's sight.
And now, in quick succession,
The gleaming steel is thrust,
The blood and foam are mingling
Upon the greedy dust.
Just then, *Vandoulah* stumbled,
And poor old *Bob* was thrown :
He lay quite pale and senseless
Without, or cry, or moan,
With savage rush the dauntless boar
Made at him, but in vain.
Again, brave *Jamie's* spear he feels,
He champs his tusks, he totters, reels
Upon the gory plain.
He panted, struggled, still no cry,
Still glares defiance from his eye.
Blood flecks his lips ; he droops his head,
And the grand old fighting boar is dead.

That night we filled the brimming cup,
And drank it with a cheer,
To our fav'rite sport " PIG STICKIN,"
And a tussle for FIRST SPEAR.

THE BENGAL THANNADAR.

Written for the *Indian Charivari*.

"LET others sing the praise of wine,
 Of women, wit, or war;
A nobler theme than these is mine,
 The BENGAL THANNADAR!

No truer homage monarch gets,
 Nor idol on his car;
Enthroned in majesty he sits,
 The Bengal Thannadar.

His mandate wholesome fear instils,
 Brings revenues from far;
Each *hookum* now, the coffer fills,
 Of the Bengal Thannadar.

The soul of honor is his creed,
 And truth his guiding star;
He knoweth not the lust of greed,
 The Bengal Thannadar.

Who says he cheats, do surely lie,
 His hands are clear as—TAR ;
To " *burk a case*" he'll never try,
 The Bengal Thannadar.

And yet the ryots on him frown,
 And fain would " *lathee mar ;*"
'Tis strange, and yet he WON'T go down,
 This Bengal Thannadar.

Foul lies and bribery with him dwell,
 He 'gainst the weak makes war ;
The truth he ever tries to quell,
 Injustice for a coin will sell :
His Thanna's oft a little hell ;
 AVAUNT THEN ! THANNADAR."

THE DAWK BUNGALOW KHANSAMMAH.

From the *Indian Charivari.*

THE shades of murdered kids around me float,
 With odours rank, of the ancestral goat:
The clarion shrill, of ancient chanticleer,
Just entered on his twenty-second year.
The leathery carcass of a slaughtered fowl,
(As lank and fleshless as a church-yard ghoul,)
From whose poor skeleton the scanty breath
Hath just been banished by " *a sudden death.*"
The fœtid odour of a stinking fish,
The sickening fumes of garlic in the dish:
The stony-hearted 'taters—and the milk
As mild and watery as Sir Charles Dilke.
The beer-stained table, thick with dirt and grease ;
The flies that left me not a moment's peace ;
And insects, we'll not name to ears polite,
Order—Coleoptera (N.B.—How they bite !)
The ragged mats, and, oh ! the filthy floor !
The cobweb festoons hung around the door.
The frowsy *palkee* in the foul verandah,
Where melancholy chickens love to wander :
The maps of mustard on the table cloth,
The thousand signs of miserable sloth.
All crowd, again, before my inward sight,
All flash before me like a gleam of light.
At THY approach, thou KNIGHT of HING AND GHEE,
GRIM FILTH INCARNATE—GREAT KHANSAMMAH-JEE.

How well I mind the tasteless soddened rice,
So cold and wet, so "*filling at the price :*"
The thumb-marked saucers, and the dirt-grained cups,
The bed on which the PARIAH nursed her pups.
The fiery brandy, and the watered gin,
The quick alacrity to " *bag the tin.*"
The coffee stains ; the tea, like musty straw,
The Butter hairy, like thy hirsute jaw :
Th' anchovy sauce, with wealth of fusty mould,
The putrid pickles, quite a twelve-month old :
The furtive scowl at any extra trouble,
The stale fumes of thy wretched hubble-bubble.
Thy dog with its inevitable mange,
Thy wealth of copper when I wanted change ;
Thy fawning grin, and sycophantic look,
When " *satisfied,* " was written in the book.
Alas ! *how* changed this " Gorgeous East" must be,
When travellers are left to such as thee ?
Though now, when sickness has become a crime,
Promotion lessening with advancing time.
When arduous duties more and heavier press,
As honors and emoluments grow less :
When loyal hearts, betrayed, are turned to gall,
"And Peter's pence is given to wealthy Paul."
When men are moved like pawns upon the board,
Their rights, their wishes, feelings quite ignored ;
What matter, if poor travellers are afflicted
With a khansammah as above depicted ?

L

MY LITTLE MARE.

SHE 's a perfect little beauty; you may scan her every
  limb,
  From her handsome Arab head, to her legs so clean
   and trim.
Her arching neck, and glossy coat, and flowing silky hair—
Yes, a perfect little beauty is my handsome little mare.

She's as playful as a kitten, and as gentle as a child,
With her dark and dreamy eyes, so affectionate and mild;
You may talk about your houris, with their beauty, rich and
  rare,
Not one could hold a candle to my handsome little mare.

And yet that eye can brighten up, with ardour and with fire,
When she follows up the baying pack, as if she'd never tire;
Each cheer to hounds—each tally ho—as speeds the doub-
  ling hare,
Seems to rouse afresh the spirits of my gallant little mare.

While the elephants are crashing through the dense and
  jungly brake,
With pointed ears she stands,—what a picture she would
  make.

How she quivers with excitement, when the tusker leaves
    his lair ;
Then bounds off like an arrow, my splendid little mare.

O'er ditch and bank, thro' waving grass, with long and easy
    stride,
We've caught him up—his tushes gleam—now we are side
    by side,
She meets his charge as firm's a rock, no trepidation there,
And seems to share my conquest, does my gallant little mare.

You should have seen her when she won the C. B. steeple-
    chase ;
So gently trotted to the post, so quietly took her place !
Great Nimrod! how the ditches yawned ; how stiff the fences
    were,
Yet she never made a blunder, did my noble little mare.

Eleven faced the starter, but five lived to the wall,
The fav'rite leading, free and strong, but here pride had a
    fall ;
Three reached the last fence—one got o'er, and with a " stun
    to spare,"
Came cantering up the winner, Sirs—my perfect little mare.

You may " *buck* " about your walers, or your "*fancy*" from the
    cape,
And rave about your Arab, with his blood, and fire, and shape
For a perfect little charger, but one the palm can bear,
' Tis a C. B. little darling, like my rattling little mare.

THE KOOKA EXECUTIONS.

The following verses were published in the Saturday Evening's *Englishman*, and I think are a fair index of the general public feeling when the first news reached us of the action of Government in the case of Mr. Cowan. At all events, they express my own opinion, and I have seen no reason since to change it.

YE shades of brave Sir Colin!
Of Nicholson! and Neill!
I'm thinking of the pangs of shame
Your gallant spirits feel!
I'm thinking of the times when waved
On high your gleaming steel—
Ere yet the British Rule was called
"The Raj of the Vakeel!"

I'm thinking of the rebel hordes
Ye hunted down to death,
Scattering treason like the chaff
Before the north wind's breath.
How your firm decisive ACTION
Conspiracies would scathe,
And England meant the wide world o'er
High valour—loyal faith.

When Energy and Firmness
Earned honorable fame,
And brain to plan, and hand to strike,
Were counted not a shame;

When men shrank not from DUTY,
Bring it praise, or bring it blame,
And English power and English faith
Were more than but a name.

When a duty rose before you,
And stared you in the face,
And you did that duty boldly,
And 'twas counted no disgrace.
Ere yet RED TAPE had held us
In its choking tight embrace,
And *Exeter Hall Philanthropy*
" Wasn't entered in the race."

When, if a rebel dared to raise
His treasonable hand,
On legal quips and quibbles,
Ye'd ne'er have made a stand ;
But quick, as from its scabbard,
Had flashed your gleaming brand ;
Ye'd have STRUCK, and thus have satisfied
Your Duty's stern demand.

But now, when gloomy discontent
Is brooding o'er the land,
When a mighty prince has fallen
By the fell assassin's hand ;
When by Kookas and Wahabees
Rebellion's flames are fanned ;
The man who did what *ye'd* have done,
Is scouted, spurned, and banned.

For one grand energetic act
That stemmed rebellion's tide—
An act that England's name upheld,
Her honor satisfied.
That thrilled us, when we heard it,
With an honest glow of pride ;
He is cast forth, shamed, and desolate,
In poverty to hide.

For two and twenty blameless years
Of weary toil and care,
For faithful, honest service,
An honored name he bare.

   *   *   *   *   *

For God's sake, public officers,
I pray you have a care,
And speak not, think not, ACT NOT,
Lest his disgrace ye share.

But when some great emergency
Comes up before your view,
Inaugurate no policy
That's prompt, and firm, and true :
Shirk all responsibility,
No steadfast course pursue ;
One only course alone is plain,
I'll tell you what to do.

Should treason and conspiracy
In troublous times arise,

And fierce incendiary flames
Gleam red into the skies,
And lust and rapine stalk abroad
With shouts, and oaths, and cries,
Be ruled by LAW, by LAW alone—
In that your safety lies.

With Acts and Regulations
Betake you to the field,
With a promise of full pardon
To the rebels if they yield ;
A stamp affixed for duty's sake,
All duly signed and sealed,
And a mild Bengalee constable
His legal staff to wield.

And also take ye out with you
Your *Indian Penal Code,*
Of right and rule and precedent,
The firmly fixed abode ;
Of red-tape, quills, and paper,
Take one full ass's load,
And a moonshee and chuprassee
To help you on the road.

What matter, tho' around you
The bullets fly like hail ?
The LAW will still envelope you
In triple coat of mail.

Its staring cold formality
Will turn the rebels pale;
Its grand uncertainty alone
Might make the stoutest quail.

Tho' ruin and destruction
Should stare you in the face;
Tho' provinces lie desolate,
Each town a ruined waste:
Tho' e'en the very empire
Should totter to its base—
If you pant for action, well you MAY
Report upon the case.

What gained we yet by clemency,
By Canning's mild decrees,
The voices of the martyred dead
Go sighing 'mong the trees.
I hear a wail of anguish
That whispers on the breeze—
What! shall our sufferings be forgot
That YE may sit at ease?

For gallantry and daring
The times are now gone by;
We're drifting on a lee-shore,
The breakers rising high.
If you're mad enough to ACT,
You may sink, or starve, or die;

But V. C.'s grants and pensions
At *your* feet will never lie.

Rich moonshees, grasping tehsildars,
Are now our upper ten,
And income-tax assessors
Our most distinguished men.
Your *ex*-daroga of police
Is a zemindar—what then?
And our glorious new redeemer
Is Keshub Chunder Sen.

We cry up—Education,
As the mighty want we feel;
But to the *grateful* Bengal youth
We the loaves and fishes deal.
The sons of English parents
May starve, or beg, or steal;
Then hurrah for cant and humbug,
And the Raj of the Vakeel!

Hurrah for Indecision!
And yet the time may come
When a nation's sobbing voice will be
With anguish stricken dumb;
When the reins will slip from palsied hands,
All nerveless, weak, and numb,
And 'tis *then* that men like Cowan
To the front again will come.

May 16, 1872.

"A HAPPY NEW YEAR."

To the readers of the O. S. M.

ONE year more has fled down the valley of time,
    With its rich freight of memories, gay or severe;
And now to our readers, in kind homely rhyme,
    We would wish a most happy and gladsome New
        Year!

Through the grey mists of morning, when falls the cold dew,
    The quick tramp of fleet hoofs falls faint on the ear;
Though your *trials* be many, may *crosses* be few,
    And your *mount* be·good fortune this Happy New Year!

May honor and manliness *come to the post*,
    All *ropers* and *pullers* be sent to the rear;
" Fair fields and no favor ! " let this be your toast,
    And luck go with merit this Happy New Year!

May fair play and probity *put on the pace !*
    And our " honest old Indian sport" *come* with a cheer;
May the best rider win, the best horse get the race;
    Gain, second to SPORT, this Happy New Year!

May sound emulation go with you *to scale,*
  And kindly good fellowship *keep the course clear !*
With courtesy, candour, and truth, at *the rail,*
  We'll enjoy honest sport this Happy New Year!

And now to all sportsmen who come to the fore,
  With clean hands, warm hearts, and consciences clear!
We pledge them; and hopefully wish SEVENTY-FOUR,
  May be to them all a MOST HAPPY NEW YEAR!!

Calcutta Central Press Company, Limited,